STAR WARS

ADVENTURES IN
WILD SPACE
THE SNARE

CAVAN SCOTT

A long time ago in a galaxy far, far away....

STAR WARS

ADVENTURES IN

WILD SPACE

THE SNARE

READ MORE
ADVENTURES IN WILD SPACE

Prelude: THE ESCAPE
Book 1: THE SNARE
Book 2: THE NEST

EGMONT
We bring stories to life

First published in Great Britain 2016
by Egmont UK Limited, The Yellow Building,
1 Nicholas Road, London W11 4AN

Illustrations by David M. Buisán
Designed by Richie Hull
Typesetting by Janene Spencer

© & ™ 2016 Lucasfilm Ltd.

ISBN 978 1 4052 7993 2
62479/1

Printed in UK

To find more great *Star Wars* books, visit
www.egmont.co.uk/starwars

THE SNARE

It is a time of darkness. With the end of the Clone Wars, and the destruction of the Jedi Order, the evil Emperor Palpatine rules the galaxy unopposed.

As the Empire expands into the unknown star systems of WILD SPACE, the Imperial Captain Korda has kidnapped the explorers Auric and Rhyssa Graf, and hopes to use their maps and data to his advantage.

The Grafs' children, Milo and Lina, narrowly escaped Korda in their parents' ship the WHISPER BIRD, and are now on course to the planet Thune, looking for help....

CHAPTER 1

POWER FAILURE

The *Whisper Bird* was in trouble and Lina Graf knew it. As soon as she'd brought the ship out of hyperspace it had started thrashing around like a bucking bantha.

'Lina, what are you doing?' her brother Milo whined as he was almost thrown out of his seat at the rear of the cramped cockpit.

'Trying to fly straight,' she snapped back, flicking switches on the main console. Warning lights flashed on and off and, try as she might, the control stick wouldn't turn.

The ship shook, buffeting both

children in their seats.

'You think that's straight?'

'Master Milo, please!' snapped the droid that was sitting to the right of Lina, linked directly into the navicomputer. 'Mistress Lina is doing her best.'

'And what if her best isn't good enough?' Milo grumbled.

'Then you being a back seat pilot isn't helping!' CR-8R said.

CR-8R, or Crater to his friends, was

a patchwork droid cobbled together by their mother from a jumble of parts. His body was an astromech's casing connected to a hovering probot base, complete with manipulator arms that whirled in the air as he spoke. He was fussy, argumentative and exceptionally annoying, but right now, he was also all they had.

Their parents were gone. Auric and Rhyssa Graf had been explorers, mapping the unknown reaches of Wild Space until they had been captured by an Imperial Navy captain by the name of Korda. Lina had always thought that the Empire was a force for good, that it spread peace and order across the galaxy. How wrong could she have been? Korda had stolen their maps, taken their parents and tried to blow up the *Whisper Bird* with Lina and Milo inside. They were alone now, with only cranky old CR-8R and Morq, Milo's pet Kowakian monkey-lizard, for company. Lina couldn't admit it to her younger brother, but she was terrified. No matter how much he tried to put on a brave face, she knew he felt the same way too.

But for now, they had more immediate problems. The *Bird* had sustained considerable damage when it had escaped Korda's explosive charges and had only just held together in hyperspace.

'Coming up on Thune,' reported CR-8R.

Lina glanced up through the cockpit's canopy, seeing a small brown and blue planet ahead of them.

'Are we going to make it?' asked Milo, hanging onto his seat as Morq hung on to him, wailing piteously.

'Of course we are,' said Lina. 'As long as we don't fall to bits first.'

'And how likely is *that*?'

There was a sharp crack from above, and sparks flew from the console's power indicators.

'Getting more likely by the second!' she admitted, wafting smoke away from her face. 'Crater, what's happening?'

The droid consulted the *Bird*'s fault locators. 'Where do you want me

to start? Systems are shutting down all over the ship. The thrusters are overheating and life-support is critical!'

'What *is* working?' Milo asked.

'The food synthesiser is operational.'

'Brilliant. Anyone hungry?'

The sound of a small explosion echoed through the *Whisper Bird*.

'Actually, no,' CR-8R reported. 'It's just blown up!'

Lina felt like banging her head against the control console.

'We need to make planetfall for repairs,' she said, trying to hold herself together.

'Did you have to use the word fall?' said Milo.

'Why not? Because if the repulsors give out that's exactly what we will be doing!'

'Life-support systems critical,' reported CR-8R.

'*Will* you just shut up!' shouted Lina.

'Don't blast the messenger,' CR-8R replied haughtily. 'I can't help it if the ship is falling apart around our audio sensors.'

Lina swivelled out of the pilot's chair and checked the readouts on the rear console.

'There's the problem,' she announced, bringing up a holographic display of the *Bird's* engines. 'The main generator is failing, knocking out all the other systems.'

'Can you fix it?' Milo asked, his voice betraying how scared he was.

Lina had always been a natural with machines. When she was little she'd spent more time dismantling her toys than playing with them. The *Whisper Bird* was infinitely more complex, of course, but she could do it. She'd have to. With their parents gone, she was the eldest now. She was in charge.

She gave Milo's shoulder what she hoped was a comforting squeeze. 'If you help, I can.'

Milo broke into a smile and gave a mock-salute. 'Aye-aye, Captain.'

Lina grinned and turned to the navigator. 'Crater, you steer the ship. Just keep us going forward, OK? Towards Thune.'

'Forward isn't a problem,' CR-8R replied. 'Any other direction and we may hit some snags.'

'You can do it,' Lina said, opening the cockpit doors and running towards the ship's engineering system.

'Oh, do you think so? How kind of you to say,' CR-8R replied sarcastically, as Milo followed his sister, Morq wrapped around his shoulders. 'I mean, I've only been flying starships since, let me see, BEFORE YOU WERE BORN!'

While CR-8R continued to grumble, Lina reached the main hold, with Milo hot on her heels. She ran over to a ladder on the far wall and started climbing up to an access hatch set into the ceiling.

'I can get to the core through here,' she called down to her brother. 'Even if I can't get it working properly again, I can trip the back-up generators. They should supply enough power to get us down.'

'To get us down *safely*?' Milo shouted up. 'You forgot to say safely.'

'I can't promise that,' she said, reaching the hatch. 'But we'll be in one piece. Probably.'

'I hate probably,' muttered Milo, prompting a whimper of agreement from Morq. Above them, Lina pressed a control and waited for the hatch to slide open.

Nothing happened.

She pressed again, but still the small

door didn't move. Trying not to panic, she flicked the manual override and tried to pull the hatch aside herself.

'What's wrong?' Milo called up.

'It won't budge,' she replied through gritted teeth. 'The mechanism must have jammed.'

'Is there another way in?'

Lina felt her heart sink. 'Yeah, there is.' She clambered down the rungs.

'So where is it?' Milo asked. 'How do we get in?'

'*We* don't get in,' Lina said. 'I do.'

'What do you mean?'

Lina moved over to a computer screen and activated a hologram. It showed a blueprint of the *Whisper Bird*.

'The generator is here,' she said, pointing at a flashing red light at the centre of the ship. 'And the jammed hatch is there.'

'OK, so how do you get past it?'

Lina swallowed. 'You use the external hatch, here.' She pointed towards a small doorway on top of the ship.

'External, as in *outside*?'

Lina tried to keep the fear from her voice. 'Yup.'

'We're in space, Sis. You can't go outside the ship while we're in space!'

'What do you think spacesuits are for? Besides, if I don't, we'll never land safely.'

Before Milo could respond, CR-8R 's voice crackled over the comms-system. '*Mistress Lina, whatever you're going to do, may I suggest you do it quickly? The retro-thrusters have failed. We can't slow down.*'

Lina slammed her hand against a nearby comms-unit in frustration. 'Change course then. Fly us away from Thune.'

'I can't. The controls aren't

responding. If we can't change course very soon – I'm afraid the *Whisper Bird* is going to crash directly into the planet...'

CHAPTER 2

SPACE CRAWL

Thune was getting bigger by the second.

Milo sat in the pilot's seat, Morq perched on the back of the chair. Nervously, he glanced over to the screen showing the inside of the *Bird*'s rear airlock. Lina was inside, wearing one of the family's bright yellow spacesuits, the bulbous helmet beneath her arm.

'Mistress Lina,' CR-8R said into the comms-unit. 'For the last time, this is a really bad idea.'

'It's the only one we have, Crater,' came her reply.

'Let me go out there,' the droid

insisted. 'I can fix the power cell.'

'The hatch is too narrow. You'll never make it through. Besides, I need you to steer.'

'I can steer!' Milo chipped in.

'Lo-Bro, you crash speeder bikes when they're not even moving! Trust me, this is the only way.'

Milo usually hated it when Lina used his nickname, but was too worried to care right now. He just wanted his sister to be safe.

On the screen, Lina lowered the helmet over her head and locked it into place.

'Very well,' sighed CR-8R. 'If you're determined to follow this ludicrous plan...'

'I am,' Lina replied, although you could hear the nerves in her voice.

'Let's run through it one more time.'

'We can't wait any longer, Crater.'

The droid ignored her. 'We open

the airlock and you climb to the top of the *Whisper Bird*. The magna-pads on your palms and knees will keep you magnetically attached to the hull.'

'*Got it.*'

'Once you've opened the hatch, don't worry about the main core. That will take too much time.'

'*Instead, divert power to the secondary systems,*' Lina continued from the airlock. '*The retro-thrusters should unlock and you'll be able to take us down.*'

'Only when you're back inside,' Milo pointed out.

'*Don't worry, I'm not going to be hanging about.*'

'In the meantime, I'm going to try to override the repulsors,' CR-8R said, 'and stabilise the acceleration compensator. Otherwise it's going to be a very bumpy ride.'

'*It's all good,*' Lina said over the

comms, but Milo knew that it wasn't. None of this was good, not good at all. He wished he could go in her place, but knew that wouldn't help. While Lina knew about machines, Milo's first love was nature. He was happiest slopping around in a bogland; discovering new species, not rerouting power generators.

Some use he was.

'Just be careful, eh Sis?' he said, trying to sound cheerful. 'Who am I going to annoy if you're not around?'

'You annoy me,' CR-8R pointed out, only to receive a whack from Morq's tail.

'Don't worry, Milo. I can do this. Crater, open the airlock.'

Milo wondered if she was trying to convince him or herself. In the co-pilot's seat, the droid fussed with some controls before announcing: 'Airlock, opening in five, four, three, two...'

* * *

'*One!*'

Lina held her breath as the air hissed out of the airlock and the hexagonal door in front of her started to open to reveal stars as far as the eye could see. Her stomach lurched and she almost shouted out that it was all a big mistake and she had changed her mind.

The door was wide open now, only a magnetic field protecting her from the vacuum. She swallowed and pressed a switch on a control panel sewn into her spacesuit's sleeve.

'Turning off airlock artificial gravity now.'

There was a beep and Lina floated up from the floor. When they were little, their Mum used to switch off the artificial gravity in the main hold so Milo and Lina could play in zero-g, whooping and cheering as they swam through the air. Suddenly, it didn't seem so fun anymore.

'Lower magnetic field,' she commanded.

'*Magnetic field deactivated,*' CR-8R responded over the comms. With a sudden burst of blue static across the open door, there was nothing stopping her floating out into space.

Imagining her mum telling her that she could do it, Lina pushed herself forward. She grabbed the edge of the open door and flipped herself up onto the *Whisper Bird*'s hull.

This was it. She was outside the ship.

Her stomach lurched, and she thought for a moment that she was going to be sick in her helmet. *Not a good idea, Lina. Not at all.* She tried to remember what CR-8R had recited from his vast databank of knowledge.

'When performing a spacewalk, focus
on the ship, not the stars. Look up and
you will become overawed by the sheer
expanse of space. Look down and you will
see the hull, solid, dependable. Take it one
step at time and don't rush. The last thing
you want to do is slip and lose your grip.'

He was right, that *was* the last thing
she wanted to do. For an annoying droid,
he could speak a lot of sense at times.

Still clutching the edge of the door, she pressed another control on her sleeve. The magna-pads on her knees and gloves activated, her knees sticking to the hull.

'It's working,' she said out loud.

'You're doing great, Sis!' Milo encouraged her.

'Yes,' CR-8R agreed. *'But I for one would appreciate it if you could do it slightly quicker.'*

'What happened to not rushing?'

'Sorry, I should have added: 'Don't rush, unless you're about to smash into the side of a planet.'

Lina sighed. 'OK. You just concentrate on getting those repulsors operational.'

'What do you think I'm doing?' came the reply.

Lina didn't answer. Instead she took a second to get her bearings before she started the long crawl to the top of the ship. The *Whisper Bird's* wings were outstretched to either side, and she was all too aware of the planet looming in front of them. Thune looked huge now, and she could see tiny dots around the ever-increasing globe. Ships in orbit. Maybe even space stations.

Another wave of nausea swept over her. *Head down,* she thought, *focus on the hull. One step at a time.*

As the ship roared forward, she pulled herself along. The magna-pads held fast, releasing as she lifted her hands and knees only to kick back in when she slapped them back down again. She could feel the ship shuddering beneath her touch, the vibrations from the failing engines flowing through her body.

'Nearly there,' she said, glancing ahead, but before Milo or CR-8R could reply the *Whisper Bird* shook violently. She slipped, the magna-pads coming loose. All at once, she was falling back into space, the *Bird* shooting forwards. She screamed, throwing out an arm, her palm outstretched. It brushed metal, skidding across the hull, until the magna-pad held and she jolted to a halt, nearly pulling her arm from its socket.

'*Lina, are you all right?*' Milo called. '*Lina?*'

'I'm fine,' she croaked, her heart hammering in her chest. 'What was that?'

'*Repulsors have fused,*' CR-8R replied. '*The power cell is about to go critical. You have to move, Mistress Lina. Go!*'

She didn't need telling twice. Lina hauled herself forward, her eyes on the hatch. Her muscles burned and her head was pounding, but she didn't care. She needed to do this, for all of their sakes.

Reaching the hatch, she found the controls and entered a code on the keypad. The hatch opened silently,

emergency lighting flaring on in the
narrow shaft below.

'I'm in,' she cheered, peering down the
short ladder that led to the generator.

*'That's great, Sis. Now don't hang
about. We've got another problem.
Actually, make that two.'*

'What do you mean?' Lina asked,
before noticing something out of the
corner of her eye. She looked up to see
a pair of starfighters racing after the
Whisper Bird.

CHAPTER 3

PLANETFALL

'They're coming in fast,' said Milo, checking the rear sensors.

'Too fast!' agreed CR-8R.

'*Try being out here with them!*' Lina shouted over the comms.

'Get into the engineering section, Sis. Perhaps they won't–'

The fighters roared over the top of the *Whisper Bird*, zooming ahead.

'*They've gone,*' breathed Lina.

Milo sank back into his chair. 'I thought they were after us.'

'They're heading towards Thune,' CR-8R reported, 'as are we, if you haven't remembered!'

'*I'm on it,*' Lina replied, and Milo flicked between the internal camera feeds to find her clambering down into the engineering section.

'I see you. How's it looking in there?'

'*Smoky. There's been a fire. Some of the cables must have burnt through.*'

He watched her swing over to an access panel. She pulled it over to find their mum's supply of emergency tools.

'*This shouldn't take me long,*' she promised. Milo hoped not. He glanced up through the front windows. Thune was massive now and he could make out every ship in orbit.

'Those are the new-model Imperial ships – TIE fighters. They're docking with that space station.'

As if waiting for its cue, a light started flashing on the control console.

'Now what?'

CR-8R checked the readouts. 'It's the

space station. They want to talk to us.'

'Why?'

'Without answering, that's exceptionally difficult to know.'

'We'll have to ignore them. How long until we hit the atmosphere.'

'Six minutes.'

'You're joking.'

'Humour isn't part of my programming.'

Milo flicked the comms button. 'Did you hear that, Sis?'

'Loud and clear. The core is in real trouble. The transfer coils are fried, but I should be able to divert power. How's Crater getting on with the repulsors?'

'Badly,' came the droid's too-honest reply. 'The safety computer is being stubborn. It won't release the repulsors until there's a stable power source.'

The light on the console flashed again.

'They're really keen to talk us, aren't they?' Milo said, staring at the approaching space station.

'They've increased the priority of the signal,' CR-8R told him. 'If we don't answer, they might send those TIE fighters to investigate.'

'Just answer the call, Milo!' Lina

snapped over the comms. *'The last thing we need is another fly-by!'*

Milo pressed the communication control with a shaking finger. 'H-hello there,' he said, dropping his voice in an attempt to sound more like his dad. 'How can we be of assistance?'

'This is Imperial Harbour Control. We were about to ask you the same question,' replied a female voice. *'You are approaching the planet at speed.'*

'Roger that, Harbour Control,' Milo bluffed even though he had no idea what he was talking about. 'We're experiencing a little booster trouble, but will sort it out, er, now-ish.'

'Now-ish?' Lina parroted from the engineering section.

Milo glared at her screen.

'Unidentified Mu-class shuttle! Please transmit ID,' the harbour controller requested. Milo killed the comms.

'What are you doing?' CR-8R asked.

'We can't tell the Empire who we are,' Milo insisted. 'They think the *Whisper Bird* was destroyed. If they find out we're alive we'll be arrested like Mum and Dad!'

'So you're just going to ignore them?' the droid replied.

'*That won't work,*' Lina said, still up to her arms in cables. '*As soon as we're in range, the* Bird *will just send our IFF code automatically.*'

'Our what?'

'Identify Friend or Foe,' CR-8R explained. 'Every ship automatically transmits an ID code by law.'

'Lina can just override it, right?'

'*Even if I could, I'm a little busy.*'

A light flashed on the console.

'They're signalling again,' CR-8R reported.

Milo felt like screaming. They couldn't have come this far to be stopped by something as stupid as an ID code. Ahead, the TIE fighters were racing back towards them on what looked suspiciously like an intercept course.

'How are you getting on with that power?' he asked, gripping the arms of the pilot's chair.

'*Just need a few more minutes,*' Lina replied.

'We don't have a few minutes. Crater needs to make...' He hesitated, not knowing the right words.

'Evasive manoeuvres,' CR-8R said for him.

'*Not with me next to the generator you don't!*'

The TIE fighters were now so close that Milo could make out the twin muzzles of their laser cannons. 'I don't think we're going to have a choice!'

'Coming within IFF transmission range,' CR-8R intoned.

'Crater, you must be able to do something.'

'I'm not sure what?' CR-8R began. 'Even if overriding the code wasn't illeg–'

The droid froze, his head cocked to one side.

'Crater?'

'What's happening?' Lina asked.

'He's just... stopped working.'

'He's what?'

CR-8R's head snapped up again and his eyes flashed. A probe arm shot out of his body and slammed into the navicomputer. 'Overriding codes,' he announced.

'But you said that we couldn't–'

Before Milo could finish his sentence, CR-8R answered the harbour controller's call. The female voice echoed around the cockpit.

'Starstormer One, *we have received*

your transmission.'

Milo stared at CR-8R in amazement. *Starstormer One?* What was *that* about?

'IFF checks out. Everything present and correct.'

Milo stared at the comms-speaker as the TIE fighters peeled off to head back to the base. 'It is? I mean, it is. Good. So we can proceed to Thune, then... please?'

'You still need to reduce speed,' came the reply. *'Do you require a tractor beam? We could pull you into the station's hangar.'*

'No!' Milo shouted, a little too quickly, before recovering. 'Negative to the tractor beam, we have everything in control.'

He switched channels to talk to his sister. 'Lina, *please* tell me we have everything under control?'

'Rerouting power... now!' Lina reported.

The *Whisper Bird* shuddered, nearly throwing Milo from the pilot's chair. With a squeal Morq landed in his lap.

'Repulsors responding,' CR-8R said, seemingly back to normal. 'Retro-rockets firing. Acceleration compensators activated.'

'You did it, Sis,' Milo shouted. 'Now get back to the airlock.'

'There's no time for that,' CR-8R insisted, the navicomputer bleeping wildly. 'We're about to enter the planet's atmosphere. Mistress Lina, I'm closing the hatch.'

'*What? No!*'

'You will be safe in the engineering shaft during planetfall. Well, as safe as any of us.'

'What is *that* supposed to mean?' Milo hissed.

'Starstormer One, *you are coming in too fast,*' the harbour controller shouted over the comms. *'You are going to crash. Engaging tractor beam.'*

'Crater, do something!' Milo yelled.

'I am,' the droid replied. 'Firing retro boosters. Full reverse. Hold on!'

The *Whisper Bird*'s hull blazed red as it plunged into Thune's atmosphere, out of control.

CHAPTER 4

NAZGORIGAN

It was like being in an Utapaun whirlwind. You would think that not much harm could come to someone being thrown around in a confined engineering shaft, but you'd be wrong. Every twist and turn of the ship sent Lina tumbling through the air to bounce from wall to wall.

'Milo!' she cried out as she was buffeted this way and that. 'What's happening?'

There was no reply, not that she would have been able to hear it if there was. The roar of the engines was deafening and if being thrown against bulkheads wasn't bad enough, the heat flooding from the defective generator was making it difficult to breathe.

Lina was thrown up towards the closed hatch and thudded into the ceiling. She dropped back down just as a thick cable burst over her head. Hot steam sprayed out and for a moment Lina thought she was going to be flung into the scorching cloud. She'd be boiled alive in her spacesuit.

Of course! The spacesuit! That was it!

She pressed herself against the wall, slapping her palms against the metal. The magna-pads activated and she was stuck fast. No matter how the ship tossed she would remain where she was.

She tried yelling for her brother again, but Milo didn't respond. The engineering shaft shook, but Lina held on. She screwed up her eyes, trying to shut out the pain in her ears, the heat from generator becoming unbearable. She couldn't take much more than this.

Then the floor stopped quaking and the engines settled down to a deep but steady rumble. The temperature was still stifling, but at least she wasn't being thrown around any more.

'Milo?' she croaked, her throat dry.

Still no answer. Lina kept the magna-pads on, just in case, but the ship's descent seemed smooth now.

If it was a descent at all. Before the ship had started shaking, Lina had heard the harbour controller mention a tractor beam. Is that what had happened? Were they being pulled into the Imperial space station, helpless and without anyway to escape?

There was a sudden thud from below, and Lina jolted forward, wrenching her shoulders. She couldn't help but cry out.

She had hurt her shoulder just before her parents had been taken and it still ached. It had happened messing around in a swamp with Milo, when the only worry in their world had been getting in trouble with Mum and Dad.

That seemed a lifetime ago now.

Lina released the magna-pads, but waited at the bottom of the shaft. A noise from above made her look up. Someone was walking over the top of the ship, right above her head.

Who was it? She recalled the stormtroopers that had taken Mum and Dad, with their pristine armour and emotionless masks.

And the blasters. She could definitely remember the blasters.

Lina crouched down, looking out for somewhere to hide. There was nowhere, other than the internal hatch that had jammed earlier, the reason why she'd had to make the space walk in the first place. Yes!

She scrabbled across to the door, only to find that the controls were still dead. Reaching back, she snatched a fusioncutter from her mum's toolkit with shaking fingers. If she could slice through the door, she might be able to escape through the main hold – if it wasn't crawling with troopers already. It was a chance she'd have to take.

She fired the cutter's energy blade at the exact point the hatch opened above her head. Lina looked up, raising a hand to protect her eyes from the sunlight that spilled down from the opening door. She was too late. A monstrous silhouette loomed across the opening, multiple arms flailing around its body. What *was* it?

'Mistress Lina?'

Lina laughed out loud, dropping the fusioncutter.

'Mistress Lina, are you alright?'

A familiar mop of unruly hair appeared.

'Can you see her?'

'Milo,' she shouted, pulling herself up.

Her brother wafted a hand in front of his face. 'Whoa, is it ever hot in there.'

'Tell me about it!' she cried, her voice cracking.

Something squealed and jumped into the shaft. Morq scuttled down towards her, throwing his long monkey-lizard arms around her shoulders when he reached the bottom.

'Yeah, yeah, I'm all right, little fella,' she laughed, returning the hug. 'It's good to see you too. What happened up there?'

'Stand back,' CR-8R barked. 'I'm sending down a line.'

A thin fibre rope dropped down the shaft and Lina grabbed hold. She sighed in relief as CR-8R began to winch her up to the open hatch. Her body ached so much that she would never have made it up the ladder again.

At the top Milo helped her out on the top of the hull, Morq hopping over to his shoulders.

'Are you hurt?' the droid fussed.

'A little bruised and battered, but I'll be OK. I'm just in need of some fresh air,' she said. Then the stench hit her as soon as she pulled it off her head. 'Ugh! But that's not fresh.'

'Sorry,' said Milo, 'I should have warned you. This place stinks.'

Then, without warning, he pulled her into a hug. She returned the gesture, holding him tight.

'You did it,' she said. 'You got us down.'

'To be honest, Crater did it, not me,' Milo said, pulling away.

The droid hovered back a couple of paces. 'But I won't be requiring a hug. A simple thank you will suffice.'

'But what happened?' Lina asked. 'I thought they wanted our identification codes.'

'And that's what Crater gave them.'

'How?'

'It's as much a mystery to me as it is to you,' CR-8R admitted. 'I was searching my databank for solutions to our IFF problem, and – lo and behold – discovered a whole archive of counterfeit registration documents.'

'Counterfeit? As in fake?'

'That is what the word means, Mistress Lina. I'm glad to see all those years of schooling have paid off.'

'But how did fake codes get into your database?' asked Milo.

'Well, they certainly weren't there before,' the droid said, sounding mortified at the very thought. 'I can only suggest that they are part of your mother's data-package.'

That made even less sense. Before being captured, Rhyssa Graf had transmitted encrypted data into CR-8R's memory. The droid had been unpacking it ever since. But why did their parents have a supply of fake IDs?

'Can you tell what else is in the data?'

Lina asked.

'I'm still decoding most of it,' CR-8R admitted. 'Approximately 12% complete.'

'Why is it taking so long?' Milo asked.

'Oh, I'm sorry. I've just been busy with not crashing. Remember? When I saved all our lives?'

Ignoring the droid, Lina turned around to take in the scene. The *Whisper Bird* had landed in a busy spaceport. Across the banks of starships sat a large town, full of tall stone buildings.

'Ow!' Something stung the back of her neck. She swatted her hand against the skin and came away with a squashed bug in her palm.

'Oh, yeah, forgot to say,' Milo said, waving a buzzing fly away from his face. 'There are insects everywhere, here. They're brilliant. Other than all the biting and the stinging. That's a bit annoying.'

'You need some bug spray, yes?' said a voice from below. The children looked down to see a large and wrinkled alien bobbing around on a personal hover-saucer a metre from the ground.

'Who's that?' Milo asked.

'Activating lecture mode,' CR-8R announced. 'It appears to be a Jablogian,

a native of Nar Kanji. Observe the blemished red skin, the beady yellow eyes and the rolls of unsightly blubber.'

'You might also want to observe the pointed ears,' the alien shouted up, 'that can hear every word that rust-bucket of yours is saying! Unsightly blubber indeed!'

'Sorry!' Milo called down, giving CR-8R a kick. 'He didn't mean to offend.'

'I can assure you that I did,' the droid sniffed. 'You'll never meet a more dishonest bunch of reprobates.'

'What was that?' the alien bellowed.

'He said he's sorry,' Lina shouted down. 'And that he's an idiot!'

'Of all the cheek,' blustered CR-8R. 'I save your lives and this is the thanks I get.'

'He's never going to let us forget that, is he?' Milo groaned.

'Just shut up and take us down to

the ground,' Lina said, climbing onto CR-8R's hovering base. 'I've had enough of being up here, one way or another.'

'What do you think I am?' the droid complained. 'A glorified elevator? Oh, very well. I suppose you'd better hop on as well, Master Milo, although that flea-bag of a monkey-lizard can find his own way down.'

In response, Morq jumped on CR-8R's head, and, grumbling, the droid floated them all down to the ground.

'That's better, yes?' said the Jablogian. 'No need for all that shouting. Welcome to Thune spaceport.'

'Thanks,' said Milo, jumping off CR-8R, only to find himself menaced by another buzzing insect. 'I think.'

'It's a beautiful place, Thune,' the alien told them. 'Except for all the bugs. It's the canals you see; the entire place is built on them. There's something in the water that attracts insects.'

'Lots of insects,' groaned Lina, swatting her neck again.

'Which is why you need this,' the alien said, producing a can of spray. 'Nazgorigan's patented bug repellent. Guaranteed to make the little critters buzz off. How many would you like?'

'Sorry?'

'How many would you like to buy? You won't get far on Thune without a can or seven. Unless you like scratching until you're raw, yes?'

'OK, we'll take one,' said Milo, fishing a credit chip from his pocket. 'How much?'

'Four credits each.'

'Four credits? That's a bit expensive!'

'Buy two get one free?' the alien suggested, pulling two more cans from his pack.

An insect landed on Milo's nose.

'Fine, give them here.'

'Good to do business with you, yes?' said the alien, handing over the cans and snaffling Milo's chips into a leather purse. 'Don't forget, if you need more just call my name and I'll come running.'

'Your name?' asked Lina.

'Nazgorigan,' the alien said, his lips pulling back into a repulsive yellow-toothed grin. 'Like it says on the tin. Tatty-bye.'

And with that, Nazgorigan was off, hovering towards more potential customers.

Milo shook the can and sprayed the contents over him, only to find himself choking a second later.

'Yuck!' he gagged. 'It's vile.'

Lina turned away, trying not to laugh. 'You smell worse than usual. And I thought that stuff was supposed to keep the bugs away?'

Sure enough, the flying insects were swarming around Milo now.

'Give me that,' said CR-8R, snatching the can from Milo's hands with a manipulator arm. 'I'll just spray a little on to my sensor and...'

The droid let out a series of bleeps as he analysed the sample.

'I thought so,' he finally said. 'You've just sprayed yourself with stagnant water, probably from the canal system.'

'What?' Milo spluttered. 'He conned me!'

'I told you that Jablogians were dishonest. If I had been allowed to continue I would have added untrustworthy, unscrupulous and downright criminal.'

Nazgorigan was half way across the spaceport now, spraying himself with what was obviously a can of genuine insect repellent!

'We come to all the best places,' moaned Milo, trudging up the *Bird*'s ramp. 'I'm going to wash.'

'There's a first time for everything,' Lina teased. 'And while you do that, I'll work out what we're going to do next...'

CHAPTER 5

THUNE CITY

'I still reek!' complained Milo, drying his hair as he walked into the *Whisper Bird*'s hold.

'No comment,' replied his sister, who had her head stuck in the workings of a small holo-table.

'What are you doing?'

'Just making a few adjustments. Crater won't let me near the generator again. Says it's too dangerous for a mere human.'

'Quite right,' came CR-8R's muffled voice from the engineering section.

Milo ignored the droid. 'So you decided to take your frustrations out on the holo-table?'

Lina replaced the table's access panel. 'I'm going to contact Dil and don't want anyone listening. I've rigged up the transmitter so the signal can't be traced back to the *Bird*.'

'Clever.'

Lina smirked. 'I know I am.'

Milo threw his towel onto a nearby seat, where it landed wetly on a sleeping Morq. The monkey-lizard squealed as he woke up.

It had been ages since the children had seen Dil Pexton. The alien was their mum and dad's agent on Thune, a Sullustan who helped the Grafs sell any holo-maps and data they gathered while exploring Wild Space. He'd been a friend of the family since before Lina and Milo were born. If anyone could help them track down their parents, it was Dil.

'So what are you waiting for, genius?' Milo said. 'Give him a call.'

Lina keyed in a code and transmitted, waiting for Dil to respond. Amazingly, the Sullustan answered immediately, a glowing hologram of his face appearing in the air above the table.

'*Lina. Milo!*' the alien said, his large black eyes widening. Like all of his race, Dil Pexton had a domed head, oversized ears and thick jowls around his mouth

that wobbled when he spoke. *'Thank the Warren Mother that you're safe. I've been worried sick. Your father hasn't been answering my messages.'*

'Mum and Dad have been taken, Dil,' Lina told the hologram. 'By the Empire.'

'They've what?'

Lina told him everything that had happened, how they'd found their parent's camp deserted and discovered a holo-recording of their parents being kidnapped.

When she'd finished, Dil frowned. *'This Imperial officer. Was it Captain Korda?'*

The name made Milo shiver. Korda had come to the swamp world they had been exploring, demanding that their mum and dad hand over all of their data. He was terrifying, a huge brute of a man with a hideous robotic jaw.

Lina nodded. 'But we don't think that

Mum gave him everything he wanted. She sent us a batch of encrypted files before she was arrested.'

'*What kind of files?*'

'We don't know yet, but we're working to decode them.'

'*No!*' Dil snapped. '*That could be dangerous. Bring them to me. I'll have a look and see what they are.*'

'What we really want to do is find Mum and Dad. We think they've been taken back to the Core Worlds, but can't be sure. Do you think you can find out?'

'*That shouldn't be too difficult,*' Dil considered. '*I know a few people in the Imperial Navy. I could call in some favours. Where are you?*'

'On Thune,' Line replied.

Dil's mouth dropped open. '*You're here? Oh, that's wonderful news. Come and see me, and we'll see what we can do. Here, I'll send you my location.*'

The holo-table gave a beep and a map appeared on the small screen set into its surface.

'Got it,' Lina told him.

'*Good girl. Follow the red dot.*' The Sullustan sighed. '*I'm really sorry about all this, kids.*'

'It's not your fault, Dil.'

'*Yes it is, Lina. I sent the Imperials to see your parents. I thought it would be a good deal for them – for all of us. I should have known. There was something about Korda that I that didn't like from day one.*'

'Can't say I'm too fond of him either,' Milo admitted.

Dil gave a comforting smile. '*We'll find them Milo, I promise. Just remember–*'

The hologram fizzed, Dil's face distorting with static.

Lina worked the controls, trying to clear the interference. 'Dil? Dil, can you hear me?'

The image of their friend solidified for a second, before vanishing, the holo-projector cutting out.

'What happened?' asked Milo.

Lina checked the controls again. 'We lost the signal. I'll call him back.'

This time there was no response.

'Something wrong with the transmitter?'

'Possibly. Crater? Have you done anything to the comms-relay?'

The droid hovered down from the engineering hatch. 'I don't think so. It's a real mess up there. I'll be able to get the *Whisper Bird* operational again, but it'll take time.'

'In which case, I'll go and see Dil,' said Milo, Morq hopping up onto his shoulder.

'You will?' said Lina.

'Well, yeah. You can help Crater.'

'I am quite capable of repairing the

ship on my own, thank you very much,' the droid replied.

'Milo, you can't go on your own,' Lina said. 'It's not safe.'

'I'll be fine. Morq will come with me, won't you boy?'

The monkey-lizard puffed out his narrow chest, trying to look brave, and nodded.

'No, I'll go instead,' Lina insisted.

'Lina!'

'No arguments, Lo-Bro. Until we find Mum and Dad, I need to look after you. They'd never forgive me if something happened.'

'It's not going to,' Milo argued. 'We'll go straight to Dil's office, I promise.'

'You're always getting lost,' Lina pointed out. 'I'm going, and that's that. Crater, you carry on the repairs. I'll talk everything through with Dil and let you know what he says.'

Milo crossed his arms, his mood blackening. 'What about the files?'

'Crater can transmit them later.'

'I don't think that's a good idea,' the droid advised. 'They could be intercepted by Imperial agents.'

'I'll send for you then. Either way, you're staying here, Milo.'

She turned to leave and Morq leapt from Milo's shoulder to land on Lina's back. She laughed. 'You coming too, boy?'

The monkey-lizard gave an excited trill.

'Traitor,' Milo hissed.

'It's probably got more to do with the fact that Dil always gives Morq loads of treats.' The animal clicked his beak and cheeped happily. 'Right, does everyone know what they're doing?'

'Yeah,' moaned Milo. 'Absolutely nothing!'

'Don't worry, Master Milo,' said

CR-8R. 'You can watch me work, if you stay nice and quiet. You may even learn a few things.'

'I doubt it,' Milo growled as he watched his sister walk from the hold.

CHAPTER 6

DIL PEXTON

Lina was glad to have Morq with her as she walked through Thune City. She had downloaded Dil's map onto a datapad, but was trying not to stare too much at the display. The last thing she wanted to look like was a tourist. Narrow streets ran alongside the foul-smelling canals, the pavements packed with aliens of all shapes and sizes. Lina had to weave in and out of the crowd, negotiating her way around the busy market stalls and jumping out of the way of the speeder bikes that zoomed up and down with little regard for the wandering pedestrians.

There was noise everywhere, from
the boats that chugged along the canals
belching thick fumes into the already
nauseating air, to the shuttles that
roared overhead. At one point, a trio
of TIE fighters had swept low over the
imposing buildings, and Lina had been
convinced that they were looking for her
and her brother.

And all the time, bugs and flies buzzed
around her, looking for a tasty snack.

'These things are disgusting,' she said,
slapping them away. She didn't expect
Morq to reach into her shoulder bag and

pull out a long silver canister.

'That's Nazgorigan's insect repellent!' she exclaimed, recognising the tube. 'The real one, not the stuff he sold Milo. How did *you* get it?'

Morq tried to look innocent. Lina laughed.

'You little thief, Morq. Although this time I won't complain.'

Taking the canister from the monkey-lizard, Lina gave herself a quick blast of the repellent. The effect was instantaneous, the insects keeping their distance.

It wasn't long before they found Dil's address. Like the others along the street, the building was made of a dirty yellow stone, rising three storeys into the muggy sky. Lina walked up to the doors and pressed the buzzer. A camera set into the porch swivelled to look at her. There were a series of beeps and the door slid open.

Morq hugged her close as she stepped over the threshold, entering a dingy lobby. Dust motes swirled in what little light squeezed through the narrow windows, and the entire place smelt musty, patches of moss creeping up the stained walls. Why was Dil working in a dump like this?

A screen in the wall flickered on, Dil's face filling the display. *'Lina, I'm so glad you came. Take the platform up to the top floor.'*

Before she should answer, the picture disappeared again. With Morq whining nervously, Lina stepped onto an elevator platform. With the sound of grinding gears, they rose steadily up an open shaft. The second floor looked deserted, but light spilled out of an open door on the third.

'Don't worry, Morq' Lina said,

stepping from the platform and crossing the small landing. 'This must be it.'

She opened the door and found herself in a large room. The only furniture was a rickety old desk in the corner and a pair of chairs, while the ancient-looking air-conditioning unit in the ceiling did little to cool the place down. At least the wooden slats across the windows kept a little of the street's oppressive heat at bay.

'Hello?' Lina said, creeping into the room. Dil was nowhere to be seen, until a door slid open to her right and the alien bustled in.

'I'm sorry Lina, I was just dealing with a little business.'

He rushed over to her and gave her an awkward hug, Morq jumping from her shoulders to scamper over to Dil's table.

'Ah, I know what you're after,' the

alien chuckled, walking towards the eager animal. He opened one of the drawers and pulled out a small bag. 'Dried clip beetle?'

Morq snatched the bag from Dil's podgy hands and dived in, cramming a purple-shelled bug into his mouth, his tiny pointed beak crunching the shell. Lina pulled a face.

'Oh, they're quite delicious,' Dil said, ushering her towards one of the chairs. 'Taste like colo clawfish. You should try one!'

'No thanks,' Lina said, sitting down. 'I'm not that hungry.'

Dil leant forward on his desk. 'It'll be all the worry. I'm so sorry about your parents, Lina.' He glanced out into the corridor. 'No Milo with you?'

'He's still with Crater. You know Milo. He gets lost getting out of bed in the morning.'

Dil laughed, activating the computer on his desk. 'What I don't understand is how you got past the planetary defences? If they thought the *Whisper Bird* was destroyed–'

'That was Crater. He transmitted a fake ID, overriding the IFF.'

'But how did he get hold of...' Dil's voice trailed off, before his eyes widened. 'Of course.'

'What?'

'A couple of years ago, I did a deal with a Trandoshan smuggler. Your dad was furious, but as payment I received a stash of fake ship IDs. I sent them on to Auric, just in case.'

'And they were in the data Mum sent to Crater!' Lina realised.

Dil nodded. 'If she was about to hand over files to Korda, the last thing she'd want him to find was a bunch of dodgy IFF codes.'

'Crater's search must have activated them.'

'I told your dad they'd come in handy.' Dil looked at his computer screen. 'Now, I've made some inquiries, and I'm afraid no one's heard anything about your parents.'

Lina's shoulders slumped. She had been sure Dil could help. The alien noticed her expression, and tried his best to cheer her up.

'There's no need to look so sad. I've only just started. Besides once you give me the rest of those files, I'm sure we'll get somewhere.'

Lina's eyes narrowed. 'The files? How will they help?'

Dil glanced over to the sliding door, before looking back at her. 'Let's just say that they're important. Wild Space is becoming quite a hot property you know.' He held out his hand. 'On that datapad, are they?'

Lina looked down at the pad in her lap and shook her head. 'No, I didn't bring them.'

'You didn't?' Dil snapped, a little too angrily. 'I told you I needed them.'

'Crater's still working on them.'

'Your droid? What's he got to do with it?'

'I told him to transmit them to you later,' Lina said – and Dil slammed his fist down on the table, sending Morq jumping onto Lina's legs. Clip beetles scattered everywhere, spilling onto the floor.

'But that's no good,' Dil said, his voice suddenly harsh. 'I need them now.'

Sweat was already running down the alien's jowls.

Morq scampered up onto Lina's shoulder to hide behind her head. 'Dil, there's no need to shout,' she said.

'You're scaring Morq.'

The agent stabbed a control on the desk and a holo-projector activated. 'Has Milo got them? Contact him now. Tell him to send them over, or better still, to come himself.'

Lina went to stand. 'And now you're scaring me. Perhaps we should come back later.'

Dil stood up, sending his chair crashing into the wall.

'No,' he barked. 'You need to stay.'

Clutching her datapad, Lina backed towards the exit. 'Tell you what, you ask around about Mum and Dad, and we'll transmit the files as soon as Crater has finished with them.'

'I'm afraid I can't allow that,' said a deep voice to her right. Lina spun around to see a figure framed in the side-door. He wore an olive-green uniform and glared triumphantly at her from beneath

a smart peaked cap. Worse of all was
his grin, showing the metal teeth of his
robot jaw.

'Hello Lina,' growled Captain Korda
of the Imperial Navy. 'How nice to finally
make your acquaintance. Your mother
has told me so much about you.'

Lina stared at Dil in disbelief. 'How
could you?'

The traitor stared at his desk and
shook his head. 'I'm sorry,' he muttered

weakly, but Lina didn't wait to hear any more. She whirled around, ready to run back out into the corridor, but her way was blocked by a pair of stormtroopers, their blasters aimed right at her, ready to fire.

Morq squealed in panic and leapt from her shoulders, making for the window. One of the stormtroopers turned and fired, the blaster sounding like thunder in the confines of Dil's office. The bolt hit the floor, but Morq was too fast. He crashed past the blinds, escaping through the open window. The trooper made as if to go after him, but was halted by a wave of Korda's gloved hand.

'The animal isn't important,' the Captain drawled. 'All I want is that data.'

He stalked forward, Lina backing away as he came near.

'She hasn't got it,' Dil said, quickly.

'D-don't hurt her.'

The Captain's head swivelled to take in the Sullustan. 'Hurt her? Why on Coruscant would I do that?'

'I can't believe you would sell us out!' Lina spat at Dil. 'We've known you since we were babies.'

Dil still didn't meet her gaze. 'They threatened me, Lina. I was scared. I've ... I've done some things in the past that I'm not proud of, before I met your parents. Your mum and dad straightened me out, but–'

'But his past crimes have come back to haunt him,' Korda cut in. 'It was a simple choice – betray you or spend the rest of his days mining carbonite in a Kalaan prison camp. Don't be too hard on him. He took all of two seconds to decide.'

Korda took a step closer and Lina banged the back of her head against the wall. There was nowhere else to go.

The Captain loomed over her. 'There really is nothing to be afraid of. As I told your parents, the Empire wishes to bring peace and order to Wild Space. To do so, we require their maps. It's really quite simple.'

'Then why did you arrest them?' Lina blurted out.

Korda's wolfish smile evaporated. "Your mother only gave me part of the data – maps of useless rocks. I thought Pexton might have the rest – how fortunate that you're still alive. I trust you'd like to stay that way."

Behind him, Dil stepped forward, coming to Lina's aid.

'Captain, please. She's just a kid.'

Korda silenced the Sullustan with a single glare. 'She's a criminal, like yourself.'

Lina whimpered as Korda raised a

gloved hand and lifted her chin so that she looked straight into his icy blue eyes. 'Tell me. Where are those maps?'

CHAPTER 7

AN UNWANTED MESSAGE

Lina had told Milo not to go outside the ship, so naturally he'd done exactly that. He wasn't having her boss him around. Yeah, she was older, but only by one year. She wasn't Mum or Dad.

It didn't help that he felt so helpless. When the generator had failed, *she'd* gone on the space walk, *she'd* got the engines running properly again. She wouldn't even let him fly the ship.

It was always the same. Milo will mess up. Milo will get hurt.

Well, Milo wasn't listening anymore!

Sitting on the edge of the canal, he pulled on the string that he'd been dangling over the edge. At the end of the line was an insect trap, a jar with a spring-loaded lid. A bizarre creature was crawling around its rim. It had multi-coloured wings like a Gorsian dragonfly, but the bloated body of a slimy reptile.

'That's it,' Milo whispered, urging the beast on. 'Go in the jar. Find your sweet treat.'

He had spread sugar paste on the bottom of the jar to see what he could attract and this was the best specimen yet. Of all the bugs that swarmed through Thune's thick air, these were the most fascinating, the pulsating warts on their back glowing aquamarine as they buzzed around the murky water.

The inquisitive critter hesitated and then darted inside, crawling into the neck of the jar. With a flick of Milo's wrist, the lid snapped shut and the flying toad-thing was trapped. Milo hauled up

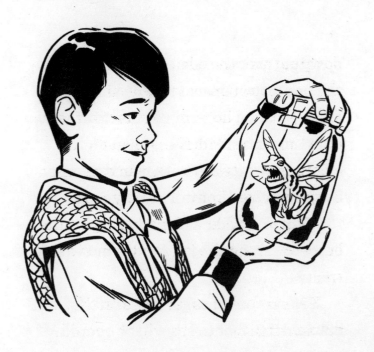

his prize, peering through the breathable
glass as soon as it was in his hands.

'Oh, you're beautiful,' Milo grinned
as the creature flitted around the
temporary prison, its warts darkening
angrily to glow a deep purple. Lina could
keep her engines and machines; he'd
take living creatures over steel hulls and
faulty power conduits any day.

Jumping up, he ran back to the

spaceport, ducking as a large bug swooped down, narrowly missing his head. No, it wasn't any old insect. It was another of the toad-flies.

Then there was another, and another, dive-bombing him as he sprinted for the ship. In the jar, the trapped creature croaked, a long tongue darting out to slap against the glass.

'Friends of yours?' Milo asked, as he reached the *Whisper Bird*, the boarding ramp automatically lowering.

Once inside, Milo placed the jar on the specimen scanner in the main hold. Dad used it to analyse new discoveries while on expeditions. Milo felt a pang of sadness as he imagined how much Auric Graf would love to see this bug.

Still, he told himself, working the controls, he'll have something to tell his parents when the *Whisper Bird* finally caught up with them. The scanner hummed, bathing the jar in green light.

'Don't worry little guy,' Milo told the insect. 'I'll let you go soon.'

A holographic copy of the toad-fly had already appeared beside the jar, mapping every part of the creature's body from its skeleton to the sacs of venom it stored in its cheeks.

Behind him, Crater descended from the engineering section. 'There you are, Master Milo. I thought Mistress Lina told you not to run off!'

'Mistress Lina says a lot of things,' Milo said, keen to show CR-8R what he had found. 'Look.'

The droid bobbed along and peered into the sample jar. 'What a fine specimen!' he exclaimed. 'A Thunian wart-hornet.'

Milo's heart sank. 'You know about them?'

'Oh yes,' the droid replied. 'Quite

common around these parts – and vicious too. You're lucky it didn't lick you.'

'Lick me?'

'It's tongue is covered in venom. Just one slurp you'll swell up like a balloon. Most nasty.'

Milo sighed. 'I thought I'd caught something rare.'

'I'll tell you all about them later,' the droid promised. 'Your father conducted a study three years ago. In the meantime, have you heard from your sister? I've recalibrated the main generator and run a full diagnosis of the *Whisper Bird*'s systems. Everything is back as it should be.'

'So we can take off again?'

'As soon as we've heard from Dil Pexton, yes!'

There was a scrabbling from the corridor, and Morq ran in, screeching at the top of his voice. He leapt into Milo's arms and clung on tight.

'Whoa, what's wrong with you?'

'What's the obnoxious runt done now?' CR-8R asked. There wasn't much love lost between the droid and the monkey-lizard.

'He's shaking,' Milo said, trying to prise the terrified pet from his chest. 'What's happened? Where's Lina?'

A light started flashing on the holo-table.

'Master Milo,' CR-8R said, pointing out the alert.

'That's probably Dil,' said Milo, running across the hold to check the read-out. Yes, the signal was transmitting from Dil's office.

'Let me,' CR-8R insisted, whirring over to the table, but Milo wasn't about to be told what to do again. Sitting down before CR-8R could get there, he punched a control to answer the call.

The holo-projector whined into life and an image appeared above the surface – but it wasn't Dil Pexton, or even Lina.

It was Captain Korda.

Morq squealed with fear and scuttled up the wall to hide in the corner of the ceiling.

'*Milo Graf, I presume,*' the Imperial officer snarled, his dark voice tinny over the comms-line. '*Welcome to Thune.*'

Milo didn't know what to do. Should he shut off the holo-projector? Should he run and hide? Instead, he chose to ask the only question that screamed through his head.

'What have you done with my sister?'

Korda laughed mirthlessly. '*An intelligent boy. I like someone who gets to the point. There's no need to worry. Your sister is quite safe. She reminds me of your mother.*'

With a cry of fury, Milo jumped up,

swinging his arm at the holographic head. It passed through, distorting the image for a second, before Korda's mocking features realigned.

'*You should apply for the Imperial Academy. We could put all that energy to good use.*'

'I'll never work for the Empire,' Milo spat.

'Everyone *works for the Empire sooner or later. We can discuss your future when we meet. That is, if you want to see Lina again.*'

Tears were stinging Milo's eyes, but he wasn't about to cry in front of this creep. 'Of course I do.'

Korda's smile fell away. '*Then send me your co-ordinates. I have to say I'm impressed. My men haven't been able to break your encrypted holo-channel and Lina is remaining tight-lipped. For now.*'

'I'll come to you,' Milo said, trying to

sound as calm as possible.

'Master Milo, no–' CR-8R started to say, but was silenced by a wave of Milo's hand.

'You want the data, don't you?' Milo asked.

Korda's disembodied head nodded. *'Intelligent* and *insightful.'*

'A public place, then,' Milo said. 'With no guards. Bring Lina and I'll bring the files.'

The officer laughed again. *'I think someone has been watching too many holo-dramas, but if you wish. What about Merchant's Bridge? Do you know it?'*

'I'll find it.'

'You have 30 minutes. If you're not there, then your sister will pay the price.'

'Don't hurt her!'

'I haven't yet, but I can and I will. That's a promise, not a threat. Merchant's Bridge. Be there.'

The signal went dead, and Korda's image vanished.

Milo sat down hard and the tears started flowing. With a mournful whimper, Morq crawled down the wall and wrapped his arms around the boy, holding him tight.

'We must call the authorities,' CR-8R said, fussing about the hold, 'and report that dreadful man.'

'I keep telling you – Korda *is* the authorities,' Milo sniffed, hugging Morq in return.

'Then what? We can't face him alone!'

Milo looked at the wart-hornet croaking furiously in the sample jar. 'Perhaps we won't need to.' He wiped his nose against the back of his hand. 'Where's this Merchant's Bridge?'

CR-8R hovered over and connected himself to the holo-table. A three-dimensional map of Thune City appeared in the air, and zoomed into a large bridge that spanned a canal. It was covered with market stalls and traders.

'Here it is,' the droid said. 'One of the biggest thoroughfares in the city.'

'How long will it take us to get there?' Milo asked.

'Only ten minutes or so, but surely we can't trust Korda? Won't his men already be looking for us?'

'They don't know that the *Whisper Bird* survived the explosion on the swamp world, and Lina's obviously not told them anything. According to your fake codes this is *Starstormer One*, remember?'

'Even so, now that they know you're alive–'

Milo interrupted the anxious droid. 'The wart-hornets. They tried to dive-bomb me when I trapped that one.'

'Well, yes,' said CR-8R, confused by

the sudden change in subject. 'They were probably trying to protect one of their own.'

'But how did they know it was in danger?'

'Now really isn't the time for a biology lesson, Master Milo. Your sister–'

Milo stood up, Morq jumping down onto the seat beside him. 'Come on, Crater. You love a lecture. Besides, if we're going to rescue Lina, now is *exactly* the time.'

CHAPTER 8

CLEAR THE BRIDGE

Merchant's Bridge was as busy as CR-8R had suggested. Milo was standing in the middle, trying not to panic. Aliens crowded in from every corner, hot and sweaty in the midday sun. The ancient bridge was wide, stalls along every side, and the cobbled stones beneath his feet were crumbling, worn down by thousands of feet over the centuries. Beside Milo CR-8R was fussing, his manipulator arms twitching.

'This is a bad idea. A very bad idea.'

'Coming to this planet was a bad idea, but I didn't hear you bleating about it then!' Milo snapped back. Morq sat quaking on his shoulders, although he jumped off when he spotted a stall selling large orange rakmelons.

Milo turned around in a circle, searching the crowd for any sign of Lina – and then their eyes met. She was standing, looking straight at him, her body rigid with fear.

'There she is,' Milo said, shoving aliens out of the way to get to her. 'Lina!'

'Master Milo, wait!'

CR-8R tried to stop him, but it was no good. The droid got caught behind a large furry monster that looked like a cross between a Hutt and a Wookiee having a bad hair day.

'Excuse me, madam,' he implored, but the alien was having none of it.

Ahead, the crowds parted enough to show Dil Pexton standing mournfully beside Lina. The agent had his hand wrapped around her arm – but if Dil was here, where was Korda?

Dil pushed Lina towards Milo and she wriggled out of his grip, running forward. She grabbed her brother and held him tight, whispering: 'Don't trust him,' into Milo's ear.

'Milo,' Dil said, trying to sound jovial. 'It's good to see you, lad.'

Milo grabbed his sister's hand and glared at the Sullustan. 'What have you done?'

Dil's ears flushed pink and he raised his palms. 'Look, I didn't have a choice.'

'Of course you did,' Lina seethed, gripping Milo's hand tighter. 'You're Mum and Dad's best friend.'

'And I'm trying to help them,' Dil insisted.

'By betraying us?'

Dil's brow furrowed, his tone hardening. 'You kids have no idea what's going on here. This is real life, not swanning around with mum and dad having little adventures. These people mean business. Don't do what they say, and they'll kill you, or worse.'

'What could be worse?' Milo asked.

'You don't want to know. Korda has enough on me to lock me up forever, but I'm not letting that happen, so be smart. Give me the data and they'll let you go.'

Lina laughed thinly. 'You don't really believe that, do you?'

'It doesn't matter what I believe, just that you've got the files. You have got them, haven't you?'

Milo stuck his chin in the air, hoping that the traitorous agent wouldn't see how scared he was. 'No. I haven't.'

'You stupid little–' Dil began, before grabbing Milo's arm and pulling him close. 'Don't you realise what you've done?'

'Let go of me,' hissed Milo, trying to pull himself free. Around them, the market-goers ignored the struggle, not wanting any trouble themselves.

'I put my neck on the line for you. Korda wanted to come marching in here with blasters blazing, but I said no, let me go alone. Milo's a smart kid, I said, he won't do anything stupid.'

'Sorry to disappoint.'

Dil's grip on his arm tightened. 'Where are they? Who's got them?'

'Unhand that child immediately,' came a voice from behind. Milo twisted in Dil's clutches to see CR-8R speeding towards them, his manipulator arms whirling to clear a path.

Dil sighed. 'Or what? You'll bore me to death?'

'Or, I'll...' The droid hesitated, before repeating. 'Or, I'll... OK, I don't know exactly what I'll do, but it won't be very nice, I can promise you that.'

Dil shook his head. 'Pathetic.'

But before he could say another word, a voice shouted above the din of the crowd.

'Time's up, Pexton.'

Dil jumped, spinning around. 'Oh no!'

'Clear the bridge,' commanded the voice.

All at once there was the sound of blaster-fire, and bolts of energy shooting up into the air. There were screams and cries of alarm as the crowd ran for cover. Purchases were thrown to the ground, while the mass of aliens almost climbed over each other to get away, the woolly female nearly mowing CR-8R down in her panic. Milo turned to his sister. 'Let's go, now!'

'Don't even think it,' sneered Dil, pulling a snub-nosed blaster from his belt. It was pointing straight at Milo.

'You wouldn't shoot us,' Milo said,

though he was not so sure that it was true.

'Don't make me find out,' Dil pleaded.

The bridge was almost deserted now, Milo, Lina and CR-8R standing in the middle with Pexton. Morq was sitting on a nearby stall, smothered in rakmelon pulp and spitting out sticky pips. It was only when he looked up and realised that everyone had gone that he jumped to the cobbles and raced over to the children.

On the far end of the bridge, flanked by a line of armed stormtroopers, stood Captain Korda. A similar row of troopers blocked the other exit. There was no escape.

As if to emphasise the point, the three TIE fighters screamed overhead, before banking and circling the city.

Korda started walking towards the children, hands behind his back. Both rows of stormtroopers also started their approach, marching in formation, blasters at the ready.

Dil shuffled closer to Milo. 'Don't argue with him,' he whispered. 'Whatever he wants, just give it to him, for everyone's sake.'

'Milo Graf,' Korda said as he approached. 'The intelligent boy with the plucky sister. Oh, they're going to love you two at the Academy.

Stormtrooper training, possibly? Maybe even officer potential. Would you like that? A uniform like mine?'

Milo didn't respond. He just stood there, clutching his sister's hand.

'Perhaps you'll meet the Emperor himself. Go all the way to the top. A clever boy like you. There's nothing you couldn't do. Your sister too. So sure of herself. So strong-willed. Not many people keep quiet when I'm asking them questions.'

He stopped in front of them, the stormtroopers standing to attention, hemming them in to the front and behind.

Milo tried to act like he didn't care. He had a question of his own.

'What have you done with our parents?'

Korda smiled.

'What have you done with my files?'

'Why should we give them to you?'

The smile vanished. 'Because if you don't, my men will start shooting. We could begin with your droid?'

The nearest stormtrooper swung up his rifle, pointing it at CR-8R. The robot gave an electronic wail and raised all six of his arms.

'Wait,' said Dil, stepping forward. 'If I know Auric and Rhyssa, they've hidden the data on that droid. It doesn't look like much, but they love that old thing.'

'Old?' CR-8R blustered, despite his obvious fear.

'Is that right?' Korda said, turning to Milo and Lina. 'Are the files in the droid?'

Neither responded, but it didn't faze the Imperial Captain.

'Very well,' he said. 'We'll strip its memory, just in case. Thank you Pexton. You have done exceedingly well.' He turned to the stormtrooper. 'Arrest him.'

'What?' Dil cried. 'You can't! I did what you said! All of it!'

'I can do whatever I want,' Korda barked. 'Drop your weapon or we will drop you!'

Dil sighed and for a moment Milo thought he was going to throw his blaster to the floor. Then, with a look of sheer desperation, he brought it back up sharply, aiming straight for Korda.

He never took the shot. Rings of blue energy blasted from the stormtrooper's rifle, knocking Dil off his feet. He crashed to the floor to lay still.

Milo let out a whimper. He couldn't help it. Try as he might, he was terrified.

'The alien's stunned,' Korda informed them. 'Nothing more. A lifetime of mining awaits him. As for you?' Korda fixed them with another unbearable stare. 'This is your last chance. Give me those files! Now!'

Milo swallowed.

'OK,' he said.

'Milo!' Lina said, grabbing his arm. 'You can't just hand them over.'

'I'm inclined to agree,' added CR-8R, 'especially as they're in my head!'

'You're more important, Sis,' Milo said, giving Lina a sad smile before turning to Captain Korda. 'If he wants the files that badly, he can have them. Crater, transmit now!'

CHAPTER 9

SWARMED

What happened next was not what Lina expected. Behind them, CR-8R emitted a high-pitched shriek, like nothing she'd ever heard before.

'What's it doing?' snapped Korda, his face contorted with pain.

Lina had her hands pressed over her ears to protect them from the sound. It wasn't working. It felt like her head was about to explode. But all the time, Milo was grinning, staring straight at the Imperial captain.

The stormtroopers shifted, aiming their weapons at CR-8R, ready to fire.

'No!' Korda shouted. 'You'll damage the files.' Then he turned to Milo. 'Shoot the boy instead. He's of no use to us now.'

The blasters zeroed in on Milo, but before any of them could fire, another noise overtook the bridge. Louder. Fiercer. The stormtroopers looked up to see a giant cloud swirling down from the sky.

No, it wasn't a cloud – it was a swarm! Thousands of bizarre insects were flying in formation, bearing down on Merchant's Bridge. Each looked as big as Lina's fist.

'Wart-hornets,' Milo shouted, above the cacophony. 'Watch out for their tongues! They're really poisonous!'

The swarm dropped on top of them. They were surrounded in seconds, the bug-things flying all around. The noise was incredible, the sound of frantic croaking drowning out the droid's

shriek. Milo and Lina clung onto each
other, while stormtroopers fired pot-
shots into the air, blue bolts of energy
briefly illuminating the dark mass that
swirled all around.

The wart-hornets reacted angrily.
They mobbed the stormtroopers,
clawing to find chinks in the armour.
They bit at their elbows, under their
arms, and behind their knees. Other
wart-hornets scurried up, inside the
stormtroopers' helmets.

Tongues shot out whenever they met flesh, dripping with venom, and the troopers began to cry out as the poison took hold. Lina saw one pull off his helmet to reveal a face that was swollen and red. Big mistake. The flying toads were on him in a moment.

Milo and Lina crouched close to CR-8R, Morq sheltering between them. A wart-hornet buzzed past her head, too close.

'It worked!' Milo shouted in triumph.

'I don't understand!'

'The wart-hornets emit a warning cry when attacked. Crater has just duplicated it, one hundred times louder than it should be. Every wart-hornet in an eight-kilometre radius has come to attack the threat.'

'But won't they attack us too?'

'Not as long as we stick close to Crater – and he keeps screaming!'

But then CR-8R fell silent.

Milo hit the droid in his metal chest. 'What are you doing? Keep screaming!'

CR-8R shook his head frantically, pointing at his head.

'He's burnt out his vocabulator,' Lina realised. A wart-hornet zoomed in, its tongue flicking out. It caught her shoulder, leaving a sticky mark on the fabric of her tunic.

'Don't let them touch your skin,' Milo yelled.

'How?' screamed Lina, and then had an idea. 'Wait!'

As CR-8R tried swatting away the flying toads with his manipulator arms, Lina rummaged through her bag.

'What are you doing?' Milo shouted, ducking to avoid a plunging hornet.

'Finding this,' Lina said, pulling a cylindrical tube from the sack.

'Is that—'

'Nazgorigan's *real* insect-repellent!' Lina sprayed a cloud of vapour over them, smothering first Milo and then Morq. 'It smells almost as bad, but does the trick.'

Sure enough, the wart-hornets backed off, concentrating on the struggling stormtroopers.

'How long will this stuff last?' Milo said, choking on the spray.

'Don't know,' Lina admitted, shaking the can. 'Long enough to get away? What's the plan?'

Milo looked sheepish. 'Yeah, the plan. I, um, hadn't quite worked that bit out yet...'

'What?'

'I got the hornets here, didn't I?'

There was no time to argue. Lina looked around and, covering her face with her hands, ploughed through the swarm to the side of the bridge. The wart-hornets parted to let her pass, but a few flew closer than she'd like. Perhaps Nazgorigan's spray wouldn't last that long after all.

She reached the edge and peered down at the canal. Spotting a way out, she called back to her brother.

'Come on you three. This way. Quick.'

In the middle of the swarm, Captain Korda was crouched down on the cobbled street, his arms wrapped around his head. His face burned and he could only see out of one eye. The pain had struck when one of these flying things had landed on his cheek. He'd swatted it away with a gloved hand, but it was too late. His cheek had started to swell, his eyes watering.

All around him was chaos, his men firing indiscriminately into the air or falling to the floor to writhe around in agony. Weak fools. Ever since he'd been a boy Korda had been blessed with a high tolerance to pain – more so since joining the Academy. He wouldn't have survived the Battle of Maraken if not. He still wore his replacement jaw as a trophy of that skirmish. A battle droid had tried to stop him then, and paid the price. These children would be no different.

But where were they?

In front of him, a stormtrooper was clutching his helmet, trying to prise it off his swollen head. Korda pushed himself up, grabbing the soldier to use him as an unwilling shield. He pushed the trooper into the cloud of creatures, trying to clear a path. It was then that he saw Milo, running for the edge of the bridge, urged on by the girl.

Surely he wasn't going to...

Korda screamed out for them to stop as, clutching his monkey-lizard, the boy leapt over the side of the bridge to plunge into the water below. The droid followed, hovering over the railing on its repulsorlift base.

Korda pushed the stormtrooper aside, not caring if the idiot succumbed to the flying toads' venom or not. Struggling to see, he snatched his blaster from its holster and took aim through the cloud of flying creatures. Half blinded by the swarm, his shot pounded into the wall of

the bridge as the girl followed the droid over the edge. Chips of stone flew up from the impact, catching the girl on the leg. She shrieked, tumbling forward.

Swatting the infernal bugs out of the way, Korda ran to the edge and glared over. The girl was floundering in the filthy canal water. Korda aimed his blaster, but before he could fire a wart-hornet dive-bombed his outstretched arm, covering his exposed skin in its venom. He cried out, the gun tumbling into the water below.

Cursing, he looked around, running to grab Pexton's discarded blaster pistol from where it had fallen. It was a cheap SoruSuub model, primitive and short-ranged compared to an Imperial weapon, but it would do the job.

Stumbling against the wall, Korda peered over the edge, but the girl was nowhere to be seen. Had she gone beneath the surface of the canal? Who knew what lived in that muck anyway?

Then there was the sound of an engine. There! The hovering droid was dragging Lina out of the water and into a small wooden boat moored at one side of the canal. Her brother was already behind the wheel.

'No you don't,' Korda spat, firing the Sullustan's blaster. The bolt hit the side of the boat, scorching the hull, but the girl was already on board. Not waiting for another shot, Milo Graf revved the engine and the boat sped forward, just as its hapless owner stepped out of a nearby building and bawled after the young thieves.

Then they were gone, thundering along the canal.

Korda slammed his fist down on the stone wall. They were already out of range of the pathetic blaster.

He looked around with his good eye, ignoring the cries of his men. Now that the droid had stopped making that piercing noise, the swarm seemed to be lifting, not that he cared. It had done his damage.

He couldn't believe it. He'd been tricked by two small children.

Cursing himself, Korda ran the length of the bridge, swatting away a hornet that landed on his chest. At the end was a civilian hunched over a speeder bike, a cloak thrown over her head to protect her from the swarm. He grabbed her shoulder and tossed her to the side. Without giving the woman a second glance, he jumped into the bike's saddle and started the engine.

The speeder bike shot into the air, scattering the remaining warthornets. Korda threw it to the left, his knee scraping against the cobbles as he turned. Gunning the throttle the Imperial captain roared away from the bridge.

Those children wouldn't escape a second time.

CHAPTER 10

CANAL CHASE

'Watch out!'

Milo slewed the boat to the right, narrowly avoiding a large barge coming in the opposite direction. The Klatooinian crew-members shouted curses after them, but that was the least of their worries. He glanced at his sister, who was dripping wet and rubbing her leg. 'Did he get you?'

'No,' she replied. 'Some of the debris from the wall hit my leg, that's all.'

CR-8R swung around, a canister of bacta-spray in one manipulator arm. Lina pushed it away. 'Seriously, I'm fine. It didn't even break the...'

Her voice trailed off.

'What is it?' Milo asked, twisting around. Lina didn't have to answer. A speeder bike was darting along the path that ran along the left-hand side of the canal, chasing them down.

'Korda!' Milo gasped.

The Imperial captain was hunkered low over the speeder's handlebars, pushing the bike's engines to the limit to catch up. Even at this distance Milo could see there was something wrong with his face. The left side was twice the size it should have been, the skin swollen painfully. One of the toad-hornets must have got him. It didn't seem to be slowing him down though. Didn't the guy *ever* give up?

Morq squealed in alarm, and Milo looked ahead just in time to avoid a collision with a small dinghy.

'That was too close,' he said. 'How far

is it to the spaceport?'

Lina pulled out her datapad and activated the map. 'I don't know where we are!'

'Neither do I!'

'You found the bridge, didn't you?'

'Coming from the opposite direction! You're the one who told us to jump into the boat!'

The datapad gave a beep as it pinpointed their location. 'Left!' Lina shouted. 'Turn left.'

'When?'

'Now!'

'A little warning would be good next time,' said Milo, pulling their stolen boat into another sharp turn. They lurched to the left, spraying foul smelling water over unfortunate passers-by on the canal's edge.

There was no time to shout an apology. Korda had crossed a bridge and

was still on their trail. He was steering
with one hand, the other pulling from
something his belt.

'He's got a blaster!' Lina cried as the
officer aimed and fired. The bolt hit
the stern of their boat, sending wooden
splinters flying everywhere.

Milo weaved around the other
boats on the canal – or at least, that
was the plan. With a sickening crunch,
he clipped the side of a barge, nearly

throwing CR-8R overboard.

'Are you trying to sink us?' Lina yelped. Morq jumped up and grabbed her head, his arms around her eyes.

Another blaster bolt struck the boat, dangerously near the outboard engine that was propelling them through the water.

'No, but Korda is. Where now?'

'I can't see,' said Lina, trying to prise the terrified monkey-lizard's grip away from her.

Milo looked round at them. 'Morq, get off her. If you need to hug anyone, hug Crater.'

Still unable to speak, the droid couldn't protest as Morq sprung from Lina's head to his!

'That's better,' said Lina, checking the map. 'Take a right, then an immediate left. Korda will be stuck on the other side of the canal.'

'So?'

'His speeder won't make it over the water. He'll have to go the long way round.'

'OK,' replied Milo, 'but remember what you said about me crashing things!'

The boat skidded around a right-hand corner, Korda's blaster fire raking the water. Then Milo flung them left. Both children cried out as the boat nearly capsized, before righting itself.

'Is he still there?' Milo asked, keeping his eyes straight ahead.

Lina looked around. There was no sign of Korda's speeder bike.

'He's gone, I think.'

'Then let's get back to the *Bird* before he finds us again.'

Lina read out the directions, Milo doing his best to react. Not once but twice, he scraped against the canal walls and almost rammed a barge full of grain, but every near-collision took them closer to the spaceport.

He grinned behind the wheel. They were going to do this. They were going to get away!

Then his ears filled with a sound like a shrieking animal.

'Oh no,' said Lina.

'What?' Milo said, looking over his shoulder.

In the air above them, swooping in low, was one of the TIE fighters. It matched their speed, dropping down above the canal, so close that they could see the dark armour of the pilot through the viewport.

'Stop the vehicle and surrender!' the pilot commanded over the fighter's loud speakers.

'What do we do?' Milo asked.

'We ignore him and carry on,' came

Lina's reply.

'Ignore the big ship with the laser cannons?'

'It's not that big,' Lina lied.

'Yeah, when you're in a Star Destroyer, not a speedboat!'

He pulled the boat around another corner, the TIE fighter following.

'Repeat,' boomed the pilot. *'Stop or I will shoot!'*

'He won't,' Lina insisted. 'You heard Korda on the bridge. They can't risk hitting Crater.'

Green energy bolts slammed into the canal on either side of the boat, raising clouds of steam as the blaster cannons vapourised the water.

'Want to tell *him* that?' screamed Milo.

Lina pointed ahead. 'Go down there.'

Milo's eyes widened when he saw where Lina meant. It was a narrow stretch of water, not much wider than the boat, a loading channel for the tall warehouses on either side.

'I'll never make it,' Milo said. 'It's coming up too fast.'

'Turn now!'

'No!'

The TIE fighter fired again, churning up the water, not trying to hit the boat but to scare them into stopping. Instead, Lina leant forward. She grabbed the steering wheel and yanked it to the right. The boat jack-knifed across the canal and crashed into the loading channel, bouncing off the narrow walls.

Instinctively the TIE pilot turned to follow them, and realised his mistake too late. Not able to make it through the gap, the starfighter ploughed into the warehouse, shearing the solar panels from its sides and exploding into a ball of fire. Burning debris rained down, hissing

as it hit the cold water.

Milo grabbed the wheel from his sister, but the boat stalled, drifting to a halt. 'What's happened?'

Lina crawled over to the engine. A neat circular hole was burned through the casing. 'It's dead. One of Korda's shots must have hit it. The fuel's been leaking out – we're lucky it didn't explode.'

'Then what are going to do? Swim?'

Lina turned to CR-8R. 'Crater, you'll have to use your repulsors.'

The droid boggled back at her mutely, shaking his head.

'Look,' she said, thrusting the datapad into his face. 'We're only a couple of blocks from the spaceport. Point your repulsors over the back of the boat and push us. Come on, Korda could be here any moment!'

The droid shook his head, refusing point blank –

A gauntleted hand grabbed the back of the boat.

Lina cried out as the downed TIE fighter pilot tried to pull himself up from the water. The black figure reached out for Lina, her terrified face reflecting in his mask's goggles.

'Crater, stop arguing and do it!'

As the TIE pilot struggled to haul

himself on to the rocking boat, the droid threw his base over the stern. Gripping the edge of the boat with his manipulator arms, CR-8R fired his repulsors straight in the TIE fighter pilot's face.

The boat shot forward, faster than before, the pilot losing his grip and flying backwards into the water.

Milo turned out of the channel and onto a clear stretch of canal.

'Keep going forward,' Lina instructed, consulting the map, 'and then take a right next to that landspeeder dealer.'

Milo did what he was told, CR-8R's repulsorlift unit whining in protest. Ahead of them the buildings on either side of the canal thinned out to reveal a cluster of large ships.

'It's the spaceport!' Lina cheered.

Milo turned to look at her.

'Yeah, and Korda too.'

The captain was standing on a low bridge ahead of them, his blaster aimed and ready to fire!

CHAPTER 11

BLAST OFF!

'Stop. Right. There!' Korda bellowed.

'I don't think so,' hissed Milo.

'What are you going to do?' asked Lina.

'This,' Milo said, twisting the steering wheel. 'Give us one last boost, Crater!'

The boat rocketed forward, hitting a row of stone steps that led up from the water. They shot into the air, soaring over the bridge and right above Korda. The captain twisted up, firing his blaster. The bolts thudded into the bottom of the boat, bursting through the deck to narrowly miss Lina and Milo – but they were away. Never to float again, the

boat crashed down onto the canal bank, shattering on the flagstones. It skidded across the street, demolishing a market stall.

Korda sprinted from the bridge, but by the time he'd reached the ruined stall, the children were gone.

'Quick,' Lina urged, racing through the parked spaceships.

'No kidding,' replied Milo, carrying

Morq in his arms. CR-8R followed behind, steam venting from his overworked repulsorlift projectors.

The *Whisper Bird* was just ahead. Lina fished out her datapad, hitting the control that would open the loading ramp. Behind them, Korda was catching up, running surprisingly fast for such a big man.

'We'll never make it,' gasped Milo. Korda was almost on them. Ahead, the ramp was down, the *Bird*'s newly repaired engines automatically powering up.

Suddenly, a figure appeared in front of them, bobbing about on his floating saucer.

'Hey!' said Nazgorigan, 'that's the lizard that stole my spray!'

'Sorry, can't stop!' Lina yelled as they dodged around the angry con artist. Behind them, Korda didn't have time to react and slammed into Nazgorigan, knocking the alien from the saucer. Imperial officer and Jablogian rolled along the ground, a mass of furious arms and legs.

It was the chance the children needed. They charged up the ramp, CR-8R bringing up the rear even as Korda tried to untangle himself from the plump alien.

'How fast can we take off?' Milo asked as they tore into the cockpit. Lina threw herself into the pilot's seat and started flicking switches.

'Already disengaging the landing gear.'

CR-8R pulled himself into the co-pilot's position, linking up to the navicomputer while trying to fix his own speakers at the same time.

'Hold on!' said Lina, and pulled back on the control stick.

'Get off me,' snarled Korda, kicking Nazgorigan from him. The alien rolled to the side, but it was too late. The ground vibrated as the *Whisper Bird*'s engines fired, blasting the ship into the sky.

'No!' Korda roared, jumping to his feet. 'Vader will have my head!'

He couldn't let them get away. The captain snatched the communicator from his belt.

'Korda to Harbour Control. Enemy ship on escape vector. Form a blockade!'

'Haven't you forgotten something?' Milo asked as Morq trembled almost as much as the engines.

'What?'

'That space station up there, and all those ships. I bet they don't think we're *Starstormer One* anymore.'

Lina jumped out of the pilot's seat.

'Then let's find out if they know we're coming. Take the controls!'

Milo blinked. 'Me? Really?'

Lina moved to the rear control station. 'You managed to steer a boat, Lo-Bro. The *Bird* should be a piece of cake.'

Milo froze, overwhelmed. Lina grabbed his hand. 'You can do this. You saved me. You saved all of us.'

'You sort of helped save yourself.'

'That just means that we're a great team, right?'

Milo broke into a grin and took his sister's place behind the control stick.

'So what are you planning?' croaked CR-8R.

'You've got your vocabulator working,' Lina said, accessing the ship's communication array. 'Pity.'

'Excuse me for wondering how we're not going to be blasted into space dust!' the droid complained.

Lina worked the controls as Milo blasted them higher into the atmosphere. 'Dad used to listen to official channels to pick up tips for new planets to explore. If I can just find the Imperial frequencies...'

The computer made a distinctly unhelpful sound.

'I can't do it,' Lina groaned, trying again. 'I thought it would be easy, but–'

'It is if you know how,' CR-8R insisted, 'Allow me.'

The droid extended another probe into the navicom. 'Accessing comms channels.'

Voices started to babble over the cockpit speakers, Imperial forces communicating across space.

'Enemy ship approaching.'

'Initiate defence grid gamma.'

'Maximum alert. Fighters scramble.'

'What are we going to do?' asked Milo,

looking back at his sister. For once, she didn't have an answer.

'I have an idea,' said Crater. 'If I track the fleet's communication relays I can triangulate their positions.'

'I have no idea what you just said,' Milo admitted, 'but it sounded impressive.'

'It is,' Lina said, realising what CR-8R was suggesting. 'Crater can work out where the ships are from their transmissions and find a gap in the blockade big enough for you to fly through! It's brilliant!'

'I have my moments,' CR-8R said, making his calculations as the transmissions kept spilling out of the speakers.

'Time to intercept. One minute 47.'

'Do you have them? Repeat: do you have them?'

'*...remember, you can resist the*

Empire. For your families, your freedom, your very future...'

'Wait,' said Milo. 'What was *that?*'

'It doesn't sound like the Empire.' Lina checked the transmissions. 'It's not even an official Imperial frequency.'

'What do you mean?'

'It's – I don't know – piggy-backing on the official channels.'

'Like a secret message?'

'Yeah, exactly that. From somewhere back in Wild Space.'

'But if they're talking about resisting the Empire–'

'They might help us. Crater, can you locate the source of the secret message?'

'I'm trying,' the droid replied.

'We won't need anyone's help if we can't get past those ships,' Milo reminded them. 'Do you have all their positions?'

Lina pressed a button. 'Transferring

them to the navicomputer now.'

The *Whisper Bird* cleared the clouds and soared up towards open space. Milo looked at the computer readout. Dots were appearing on a grid pattern, each representing a different ship.

'There's an awful lot of them,' he groaned.

'But there's no going back now,' Lina said. 'We've picked up two fighters.'

'Where?'

'Right behind us! Look!'

Milo followed her gaze to the display showing the feed from *Bird*'s rear sensors. Two TIE fighters had burst through the clouds, gaining on them with every passing second.

He swallowed. 'Fast, aren't they?'

'I think I've located the source of the transmission,' CR-8R reported. 'The planet Xirl, near the Kalidorn system.'

'Great, but how do we get away?'

Ahead of them, on the edge of space, the Imperial ships had formed a blockade. Behind them, the TIE fighters were locking their weapons on to the ship.

This time, there really was no escape.

CHAPTER 12

NOWHERE LEFT TO RUN

On the ground, Korda ran into his waiting shuttle. The pilot turned, his mouth dropping open.

'Captain, your face!'

'Never mind that,' wheezed Korda. He was finding it hard to breathe now, the wart-hornet venom ravaging his body. 'Emergency take off. Get us up to the blockade.'

As the pilot prepared for launch, an alarm sounded from the communication console. Korda's heart was already racing, but his pulse quickened all the more when he realised who was trying to contact him.

Dropping into a chair, he accepted the call.

A hologram of an imposing figure wearing a black helmet shimmered into life in front of him.

'Lord Vader,' Korda rasped. 'How may I be of assistance?'

'You can tell me that you have those maps,' the masked figure rumbled.

Darth Vader was a force to be reckoned with, answering only to the Emperor himself. He wasn't a man to cross.

'Soon, my Lord. We have formed a blockade, but the children–'

'Children?' Vader snapped. 'You are being outmanoeuvred by *children*?'

'We have them, sir. They won't get away.'

'Make sure that they don't,' Vader commanded, and the holo-transmission ended.

Korda fell back in his seat. He felt sick to his stomach, and it had nothing to do with the venom running through his system.

Sweating, he looked out of the viewport. If this didn't work, he was finished.

'There!' said Lina, pointing at the dots

on the screen. 'There's a gap.'

'Barely,' said Milo, although he adjusted the *Bird*'s flight pattern to head towards it just in case. 'Even if we could make it through there, the ships will be able to block our path.'

Lina thought quickly. 'Not if we jump to hyperspace.'

'When?'

'Now!'

'But we're still in Thune's atmosphere.'

'Mistress Lina,' CR-8R chipped in. 'As well you know, the hyperdrive engines won't fire within the gravitational pull of a planet. The safety protocols will activate.'

'Not if we turn them off.'

CR-8R's head snapped around so fast, Milo thought it might explode. 'You can't do that!'

Lina nodded. 'Actually, I can. When I

got the main generator working, I had to by-pass the safety cut-outs. We could do the same for the jump to lightspeed, stop the computer switching the engines off. It's simple.'

'But highly dangerous!' the droid added.

'Only if we blow up.'

'Is that possible?' Milo asked.

'Either that or the ship falls apart in hyperspace.'

The two children looked at each other.

'Then we better try it,' Milo finally said.

'What?' CR-8R screeched.

Energy bolts screamed past the *Whisper Bird*, centimetres from the ship's hull.

'That was the TIE fighters,' Milo said. 'They're firing warning shots.'

'We have an incoming message,'

CR-8R reported, sounding most put out by the entire situation.

'Let's hear it then,' said Lina.

Captain Korda's voice wheezed over the speakers. '*You've nowhere left to run! Surrender and I'll let you live!*'

Milo killed the comms-link. 'Do we trust him?'

'The only person I trust is you,' Lina told him.

Morq let out a squeak. 'And the monkey-lizard.'

'Charming,' huffed CR-8R.

Milo looked at the approaching blockade of Imperial ships. Freedom lay on the other side, and their parents, somewhere out there.

He gripped the control column. 'We'll only have one chance at this. Let's make it work.'

'Are you sure?' Lina asked.

'No!' insisted CR-8R.

'Do it!' said Milo.

Lina went back to the controls, accessing the ship's power systems and giving commands that usually the computer would never obey. There was a warning beep, and she nodded.

'Done. We can jump whenever you're ready.'

'There's no time like the present,' Milo said, grabbing the hyperdrive lever.

Before he could change his mind, he pulled it back hard.

The *Whisper Bird* jumped into hyperspace, blasting straight through the blockade. Behind them, the TIE fighter pilots were so shocked that they ploughed straight into the Imperial ships, exploding on impact.

In his shuttle, Captain Korda stared at the blossoming flames and screamed: 'NO!'

Against all odds, the Graf children had escaped. But where were they heading?

TO BE CONTINUED IN
STAR WARS
ADVENTURES IN WILD SPACE
Book Two: THE NEST